# Wrath

*and*

# Ruin

Dragon Riders of Osnen Book 14

RICHARD FIERCE

Dragonfire Press

Copyright © 2023 Richard Fierce



Cover design by germancreative.

Cover art by Nimesh Niyomal

ISBN: 978-1-958354-20-9

# CONTENTS


Chapter 1      1

Chapter 2      7

Chapter 3      14

Chapter 4      21

Chapter 5      27

Chapter 6      33

Chapter 7      40

Chapter 8      47

Chapter 9      54

Chapter 10    59

Chapter 11    65

Chapter 12    71

Chapter 13    77

Chapter 14    83

Chapter 15    89

Chapter 16    97

# 1

*You lied to me.*

Sion's words burned in my mind like a brand, and guilt assailed me.

*I'm sorry,* I said. *I thought I was doing what was best.*

Sion snorted. *Being deceitful is never what is best.*

*Didn't you tell me to lie to the wild dragons about Drakus?*

*I told you we should kill him. I never told you to lie about it.*

I thought back to our conversation and realized she was right. The path I found myself on seemed to grow darker with each decision I made. What was I doing? I ground my teeth in frustration.

*I'm sorry,* I repeated.

*Never lie to me again.*

I swallowed hard, nodding, and the silence stretched between us. She still didn't know about the orbs, but since they had been destroyed, I saw no point in telling her about them. She was already angry with me, and I didn't want to infuriate her further.

We rested atop a hill, and I stared off into the

distance. The sun burned hot, heat waves dancing a slow dance, shimmering everything in sight. We had reached the mainland late last night, and the wild dragons were exhausted. Maren and Demris were with them, resting outside the port city. I felt like we were wasting valuable time, but I knew we couldn't push the poor dragons any harder.

*Do you think the Citadel is still standing?* I asked.

*Master Anesko is a wise leader. I am sure he is keeping the king at bay.*

I hoped that was true, though it was impossible to know for certain.

*How long before they'll be ready to fly again?*

Sion hummed softly, the sound vibrating the ground beneath me.

*Give them a few hours. We can still reach the Citadel before nightfall.*

I stood up and stretched. *I'll be back.*

*Where are you going?*

*For a walk.*

I strode down the hill, and I could feel Sion's confusion filtering through the bond. I didn't blame her. The way things were going recently had me confused as well. In trying to do what I thought was best, I continued to stumble. Perhaps it was best if I didn't try to play leader. Clearly, I was failing miserably at it. And despite that, Sion and Maren continued to follow me … but why?

I reached the bottom of the hill and breathed in deeply of the air. The smell of salt water still permeated my nostrils, but the moist earthy scent of the grass did well to drive it away. I enjoyed being out at sea, but it was good to be home. An invisible heaviness overcame me, and I paused to glance around.

"Eldwin."

My eyes blurred momentarily, and then I saw a cloaked figure standing before me. Instinctively, I put my hand on the hilt of my blade.

"I see you found the Wild Ones."

It was Tyrval.

I let go of the hilt and nodded, suddenly feeling exhausted. "Yes, we did. It would have been helpful to know your brother was playing god over them."

"Drakus is still alive? I'm impressed."

"He was," I clarified. "The Wild Ones took their wrath out on him."

Tyrval didn't seem fazed by the news. She probably hadn't seen him since he'd left the mainland, which was long enough to lose any familial connection.

"After they've rested, we're flying to the Citadel."

"Good," Tyrval replied. "When that is settled, the Assembly could use some help."

"With what?"

"We still haven't found Risod. Nemryth suspects the dragon slayers have captured her."

"My hands are full," I said. "I don't know how long it will take to deal with the king, and there's no guarantee we will be victorious."

"Dark times indeed, but we must never lose hope, my boy. The night is darkest before the dawn, as the saying goes."

I had never heard that saying before. If Tyrval thought it would inspire me, she was wrong.

"Send word if you find her," I said. "Otherwise, I will seek you out later."

With a blink of my eyes, Tyrval was gone. The heaviness I felt dissipated, and I stared at the spot where she had been. Had the Assembly not asked enough of me? There were many people in this world, and yet they always requested my aid. It was enough to drive me mad.

*What's wrong?* Sion's voice interrupted my thoughts.

*What isn't?* I replied. *Everyone in this world needs help and there aren't enough people to stand in the gap.*

My words took Sion by surprise. I felt her shock for only a moment before she recovered and withdrew from my mind. I stared off in the Citadel's direction and wondered what was next. It seemed as though there was always another battle to fight, as if there was never a moment of rest before something bad threatened the world. I heaved a sigh and trudged back up the hill to where Sion waited.

*Forgive me,* I said as I crouched in front of her. She blinked at me, and I ran my hand along her snout comfortingly. *I'm in a bad mood. Maybe with some sleep, I'll be back to myself again.*

*There is more to your brooding than lack of rest. Darkness weighs on your heart. I can feel it in our bond.*

I wanted to argue with her, but I knew she was right. Ever since T'Mere's death, the suffocating weight of death and despair had slowly been clawing its way into my mind. I ignored it by focusing on everything else, and perhaps that was the reason I continued to fail. Yet if I faced the darkness, would I defeat it, or be lost to it?

*None of us are perfect creations,* Sion said.

*Not even dragons?* I asked, cracking a slight grin.

*Not even dragons.*

An overwhelming rush of emotions hit me suddenly, and it took every ounce of strength to keep the tears from falling. What kind of leader cried when things got difficult? I closed my eyes and rested my forehead against Sion's hard scales.

*You will survive this,* she said.

*How do you know?*

*Because I will flame your soul from the afterlife if you do not.*

That made me laugh, and this time, I did not

stop the tears from coming. I wrapped my arms around Sion's massive head and held onto her as tightly as I could, as if she alone could stop my descent into madness.

After a long moment, I released her and wiped the tears from my cheeks. It dawned on me that the world was much like the Path on the Island of Lost Souls. It demanded much and gave little in return, but if I had survived that terrible place, I could certainly survive this ordeal.

*Thank you for never giving up on me,* I said.

Sion nuzzled me, knocking me over backward. *Dragons never give up.*

*That is a good thing.*

*Indeed. A war is coming, and dragons will decide the fate of the Order.*

*And of Osnen,* I said solemnly.

# 2

There was nothing that burned hotter than dragon fire.

Tents and grass were consumed and stones melted as Sion breathed her flames across the small camp of royal scouts. The soldiers died silently, taken completely by surprise. I shielded my face from the heat and held my breath until Sion swooped up and the air grew cooler. The devastation made me glad I had never been at the wrong end of a dragon's wrath.

*I'm surprised Erling has scouts this far west. The Citadel is still miles away.*

*Perhaps he thinks more riders coming to aid Anesko?* Sion suggested.

*Maybe, but he knows our numbers are limited. Unless a spy informed him of our plan to find the wild dragons, I doubt he's expecting a surprise.*

Sion wheeled in a wide circle, and I scanned the ground for more scouts.

*All looks clear to me.*

*If there are scouts out here, I think they will be closer to the Citadel,* Sion said. *How will we get inside without notice?*

I'd spent a lot of time thinking about that, and

I'd decided on a path that was likely a suicide mission. I sent an image of what I was considering through the bond and waited for Sion to rebuke me. Surprisingly, she seemed pleased with the idea.

*It is full of risk, but it is the last thing anyone will expect.*

*That was my thought as well,* I said. *We just need everyone to agree. My only fear is these dragons don't have any battle experience. They're likely to cause more damage than help.*

*That is possible,* Sion agreed. *But the only ones outside the safety of the Citadel are the king's men. I say bring on the destruction.*

I smiled and patted her neck. Sion turned back the way we came and flew until the wild dragons came into view. She landed near Demris, and I dismounted and slid down Sion's shoulder, then trudged to where Maren was sitting. She looked up as I approached.

"The scouts have been dealt with," I said.

"Good. The way ahead should be clear, then?"

"I'm not sure. Sion thinks there may be more the closer we get. I could take the lead and make sure, but if we're spotted, then we'll lose the element of surprise."

"If there are enough scouts, we'll be discovered,

regardless."

"I know, but I have a plan."

Maren stared at me expectantly.

"Instead of trying to get into the Citadel, I think we should strike at your father's forces."

Just as I expected with Sion, I assumed she would argue against my idea. Instead, she nodded.

"Surprise them."

"Exactly," I said.

"It's risky."

"If we cause enough chaos, they'll retreat. That will give us the opportunity we need to get inside the Citadel without risking everyone else's safety."

"What if they don't retreat?" Maren asked.

"If they are wise, they will," I replied. "Otherwise, their losses will be heavy."

"If I know my father, he'll have his best men closest to the Citadel. They won't flee at the first sign of trouble."

"Nobody said this was going to be easy. Besides, if we succeed, we'll be trapped inside the school, but I can't think of anything better."

Maren nodded. "Once all our forces are pooled together, we can decide what to do next. It's settled, then. Now we just have to convince Getarros."

Getarros hadn't spoken to me since we'd arrived. I was certain his rage still burned hot, but without him and the other wild dragons, we didn't stand a chance against the king.

"Any ideas on what I should say?" I asked.

"I'll speak to him, but you need to be with me. He may be angry with you, but he has no reason not to follow you. If it wasn't for you, he would still be a slave to Drakus."

Maren had a point, but dragons were stubborn creatures. If he decided he no longer trusted me, there was nothing she could do to sway him.

"Let's get it over with, then."

I helped Maren to her feet, and we strode across the grassy field to where Getarros lay. The dragon was basking in the sun. He opened his eyes as we advanced, and his tail flicked back and forth in an agitated manner. He yawned as he rose to his feet, a deep growl rumbling in his chest.

"We need to speak with you," Maren said.

Getarros turned his gaze on me, and the tension was as thick as smoke. Despite the fear he instilled in me, I kept my eyes locked on his. He looked at Maren, and the two must have started talking. I reached out to Getarros, but he'd blocked me from his mind. After a long moment of awkward silence, Maren looked at me.

"He wants to speak with you."

I nodded hesitantly. I didn't think he would do anything to harm me, but I let Sion know anyway. Maren kissed me on the cheek and walked away, leaving the two of us alone.

*If you are still angry with me, I understand. I am angry with myself.*

*I am not one to brood over past mistakes,* Getarros replied.

Relief washed over me.

*You seem to be avoiding me, so I assumed—*

*It is not you that troubles my thoughts. All my life, I have served Drakus. Now that he is gone, there is a void that hangs over me, over all my brethren. At the Whispering Cliffs, we knew our place. We do not know our place here in your land.*

His words surprised me. It sounded as if he was afraid. A dragon, afraid? It was a strange thought.

*Master Anesko at the Citadel will welcome you and the others. All the riders will.*

*I do not doubt that, but your hospitality is not what burdens me. We are not like Sion and Demris.*

Getarros looked past me at Sion for a moment.

*We do not want to bond with humans,* he said.

My hopes of restoring the Order to its full glory crashed, shattering like a thousand pieces of glass.

*I don't understand.*

*I don't expect you to.*

Silence stretched between us, and I swallowed the lump that had formed in my throat.

*Without you, we cannot defeat the king.*

*Yes, I have already considered this. We will help you with your battle, but when it is done, we will leave and make our own place in this new world.*

That was a sliver of hope, at least.

*You and your brethren are the hope of future generations. Without you to strengthen the Order, it is unlikely we will survive. Once the riders are gone, there will be no one to protect the land from tyrants like the king.*

*Where there is evil, good will always rise to meet it,* Getarros said.

*Will you at least reconsider?*

*No, I have made up my mind on this matter.*

That was it, then. There was no way to force them to bond with humans. For a brief moment, I wished we still had the orbs. I immediately pushed the thought away and berated myself for even thinking that. Even if we did still have the orbs, I could never use them in good conscience, not to force the dragons into a second slavery.

*Very well. I will not press the issue. It is more than enough that you are going to help us.*

*Indeed, it is more than you deserve.*

*I thought you weren't still angry?* I asked.

*I'm not, but you have caused more pain than you know. My brethren and I must now learn to do many things. To hunt, to defend ourselves. We did not have these worries under Drakus. You may have freed us from a tyrant, but now we are prisoners to ignorance.*

I had not considered that, but I had not considered the dragons would not join the Order, either. The number of mistakes I made continued to grow. Even if we saved Osnen from the king, it seemed the Order was doomed to die out.

# 3

Maren and I sat together among the tall grass, daylight long gone. A small fire burned low, the flames dancing with vigor as if all in the world was well. The slumbering of the wild dragons filled the air, the sound like that of a strong wind.

"We have failed," I whispered.

"How so?" Maren asked, turning her head to look at me.

"If Getarros and the others will not bond with humans, then the riders will end. We are too few as it is. If Anesko was contemplating disbanding us before, he will certainly consider it again now."

Maren rested her head on my shoulder. "You worry too much."

"How can I not? And how can you be so calm about things?"

"I have faith things will work out in the end."

I laughed, but not out of humor. "Your faith is stronger than mine."

"I do worry about the future, Eldwin. I just try not to dwell on things I cannot control. We will survive whatever comes our way, good or ill."

The fire crackled, and a small flame leaped from the coals, temporarily lighting the shadows. The darkness was deep this night, and it reminded me of the feeling I experienced when Sion had been cut off from me on the Island of Lost Souls. I had seen many terrible things since then, but I always persevered. Perhaps Maren's faith was not unfounded.

"I'm going to bed," she said, lifting her head off me. "Tomorrow will be difficult enough, even with plenty of sleep."

I nodded absently, still lost in my thoughts. Maren wandered over to Demris and curled up beside him. The air wasn't chill, but the warmth of a dragon was always comforting. I leaned back on my elbows and stared up at the moon.

As a child, I had dreamed of becoming a dragon rider, following in my father's steps. He had taught me about honor and love, but nothing about dragons or the school. I still found that odd. Had he wanted me to learn things on my own, or protect me from living the same harsh life he had?

*Silence your thoughts,* Sion's voice rumbled in my mind. *I cannot sleep with your constant worries.*

*Sorry,* I replied. *I can't help it.*

I closed the bond on my end and continued to stare at the moon. It was little more than half full.

Perhaps my father's silence on the latter things was indeed because he wanted to protect me. That made me a fool, then. Not only a fool, but arrogant and selfish.

Again, my mind strayed to the coming battle. How could we defeat a king? A man so confident in his own power, he had no qualms about destroying the very people who protected his kingdom.

I sighed. It was impossible to ignore my anxious thoughts. Staring at the moon certainly wasn't helping. I stood up and walked along the field toward a small stream I had seen earlier. Perhaps drowning myself in cold water would take my mind off things. I knelt in front of the water and was about to put my hands in when I abruptly stopped and froze.

I sensed something, but I didn't know what it was. Glancing around revealed nothing but the shadowy swaying of the grass. I re-opened the bond.

*Sion?*

*I am here.*

*Do you sense anything out of the ordinary?*

There was a pause, and I heard her stirring across the way.

*Magic,* she said. *I think it's the dragon slayers.*

I recoiled from the stream and drew my sword, shifting my gaze back and forth. I thought she had killed the sorcerer. Did the other slayers know magic as well? A few moments passed and nothing happened. Sion joined me near the stream and sniffed the air.

*Whoever it was is gone now,* she said.

*You said it might be the dragon slayers. Do you think it could have been a scout from the king's army?*

*No. The feel of the magic was the same as the slayers.*

We stood guard until I grew too tired to stay alert. I sheathed my blade and followed Sion back to the camp. She got comfortable, and I lay beside her.

*I can barely keep my eyes open,* I said.

*Rest. I will keep watch.*

I fell asleep and was greeted by bad dreams about dragon slayers, the fall of the Order, and the king terrorizing Osnen. When dawn came, I awoke to find many of the dragons ready to go, eager even. Maren had prepared breakfast, and I devoured my portion quickly. Despite my fears, there was a level of excitement about returning to the Citadel. It was the only home I had, after all.

Once all the dragons were ready, we flew for the Citadel. Unlike the many other times I had returned to the school, this time felt like a march to war. There was a mixture of fear and determination in the air, and it put me on edge. Sion kept a close eye on the ground, watching for scouts, but fortune was on our side as the way was clear.

*Things may actually go according to plan,* I told Sion.

*That would be a welcome change.*

*Indeed.*

As we drew closer to the Citadel, plumes of smoke rose in the distance. At first, I thought the school was burning, but I soon realized it was only the fires from the king's encampment. Demris and Maren flew to our right, and I looked over, catching Maren's attention.

"Get ready!" I shouted into the wind.

She nodded, her expression serious. I mouthed the words 'I love you.' She smiled and mouthed them back, and I turned my attention ahead. There were countless tents outside the walls of the school, and the camp took up several acres. Soldiers were everywhere, numbering in the thousands. Banners with the royal crest fluttered from poles, and we descended toward the nearest tents.

A horn blared as someone spotted us, and the king's riders took to the air to meet us. Roars of challenge rang out, and I looked over my shoulder to see the wild dragons break formation into smaller groups. They split up and descended upon the camp, breathing fire and smashing things with their tails.

Considering their lack of experience, their display impressed me. A small group of the king's riders ignored them and came straight for me and Maren.

*Brace yourself,* Sion warned.

She spun in a circle to the left and engaged a blue dragon. The soldier on its back held a lance at the ready, the tip of the weapon gleaming under the sun. At the last moment, Sion stretched her wings out, catching the air. Her upper body lifted, sending her rear claws into the face of the other dragon. A sharp sound tore through the air as her claws scraped against the enemy's scales.

I flinched and covered my ears, gripping the saddle tight with my legs. The other dragon roared and maneuvered away from Sion, lashing at her with its tail. Sion gave chase, following the beast as it winged its way around the protective shield of the Citadel. The soldier was a skilled rider, guiding his mount left and right to avoid the blasts of flame that Sion breathed at them.

The wind whipped through my hair with every twist and turn and dried my eyes out to the point I had to shield my face in the crook of my elbow. The smell of smoke and brimstone hit my nostrils, and I risked a glance down at the encampment to see what damage the dragons had done.

A third of the camp was on fire, but the progress of the wild dragons was now stalled as they began battling the king's riders. The organization they had displayed initially was gone, replaced by chaos as their ranks broke. I watched in horror as several of the dragons were slaughtered brutally, their bodies falling from the sky and crashing among the camp.

Sion roared in surprise, and I looked up. Half a dozen royal riders came rushing toward us. The blue dragon had lured us into a trap.

# 4

The riders flew in a tight formation, their wings stretched wide to form a wall that blocked the way forward. I looked around desperately, searching for a way to escape. My heart was racing, and my mind was spinning with possibilities. We could fly straight up, but they would certainly follow us. Then I saw a gap between two riders on the right side of their formation.

It was small, but if we could get through it, then maybe we could break away from them and regroup with Demris and Maren. I risked a glance in the direction they had been, but I could no longer see them.

*Can you make it?* I asked, sending Sion a mental image.

*I will try.*

She lashed her tail with determination and flew straight for the gap. The royal riders must have seen what we were doing because they moved faster to box us in even as we approached. I gritted my teeth as I watched the riders surge toward us.

The riders pinned us down, closing in on all sides, leaving us with no way out. We were outnumbered and outmatched, and there was no way we could fight our way out of this one and survive.

A shadow passed overhead, and a moment later, Getarros and a group of wild dragons swooped in from above. Their sudden arrival caught the royal riders off guard, giving Sion an opening to make her escape. I urged her on, and she flew up as fast as she could. The wind rushed past my ears as we soared higher and higher into the sky, putting distance between us and the king's soldiers.

The sun shone brightly, its rays illuminating everything below us in a golden hue. Looking down, I could see the king's soldiers and the wild dragons battling. Getarros's group had the advantage, and they were slowly driving the royal riders back.

*They are holding their own well,* I said.

*Yes, but if the king's men coordinate their efforts, we will lose the advantage. We need to do something to force them into a retreat. It would not be wise for Anesko to lower the shield with the enemy this close to the walls.*

She was right. I scanned the encampment below. The ranks of the wild dragons had broken, the beasts scattered and struggling. It was a very different sight than watching Getarros and his group as they took down the royal riders.

*We need to rally them,* I said. *Then flame the camp all the way to the king's tent.*

*Shouldn't we target the king directly? That will end things quickly.*

*Not unless Maren is with us. It won't be that easy to get rid of the king. I'm sure he's got sorcerers nearby.*

*I'll flame them, too,* Sion growled.

*I don't doubt you would. Let's get the attention of the wild dragons. We need to bring the heat.*

Sion dove, rushing past Getarros's group, and issued an ear-splitting roar as she arced over the camp. Half a dozen dragons looked at her and winged their way to our side. Sion flew back and forth over the camp, and with each pass, more dragons answered her call, including Demis. Maren nodded at me, and I was glad to see they were safe. The royal riders broke away from the battle and pulled back, surrounding the king's pavilion.

*It's working,* I said. *The king must be worried.*

*They are regrouping. Many of the wild ones have fallen, and while we still have numbers on our side, our enemy outmatches us in experience.*

I surveyed the camp again now that we were closer to the ground and saw the terrible truth of her words. Roughly a third of the wild dragons were dead or mortally wounded. The pained cries of men and beasts filled the air, and I knew that no matter how this battle ended, there truly was no victor.

*We need to attack them now, before they recover.*

*As you command,* Sion replied.

She roared and changed direction, heading toward the royal riders. The wild dragons flew with us, and as we converged on the king's tent, the world erupted in fire and heat. Archers were positioned around the tent, and volleys of arrows filled the sky. The attack served no purpose, at least none that I could discern, and the projectiles clinked harmlessly off the dragons' scales.

Sion breathed a torrent of flames into their ranks, and the smell of burning wood, metal, and flesh seared my nostrils. The king's pavilion, however, remained untouched. The flames that came within a few feet were immediately snuffed out.

*You were right,* Sion said. *The king's sorcerers are protecting him.*

*We can do nothing about that, but we can drive his riders away.*

"Ignore the soldiers on the ground!" I shouted.

"Attack the riders!"

More arrows sailed through the air, but Sion and the other dragons were undeterred. She opened her jaws and bathed our enemies in the orange glow of her flames. The heat was suffocating, and I did my best to hide behind Sion's bulk until it was safe.

When I looked up, my hopes soared. The royal riders were retreating, leaving the king's pavilion behind. A chorus of roars arose from the wild dragons, and Sion and Demris joined their celebratory sounds.

*This is only a minor victory,* I said. *Now we must hurry to the Citadel.*

*Let them be proud. They are not warriors like us.*

Sion circled back and flew for the Citadel. The magical shield was still up, and as we got closer, I saw a line of people on the wall. Anesko's robed form was unmistakable. I waved at him, and a moment later, the shield flickered out of existence. I looked over my shoulder and motioned for the wild dragons to fly ahead.

They continued onward, and Sion and I remained outside the walls. I kept my eyes on the king's camp, but the royal riders had not returned yet. Once all the dragons were safely inside the confines of the Citadel, we crossed over the wall and landed in the crowded courtyard. I dismounted and hurried to meet Anesko as he purposely bounded down the stairs from the ramparts.

"You found them," he said breathlessly.

"We did, but it wasn't easy."

"You do not know how glad I am to see you." He stared past me. "There are so many of them."

"There were more, but we lost a lot of them in the battle. It was the only way I could think to clear a way into the Citadel."

"You were forced to make a difficult choice," Anesko said. "In your shoes, I would have chosen the same path. The risk was great, but it paid off."

"Yes, but now we are prisoners inside our own home."

"I am confident we will find a way out of this. Now that you have returned, we will convene with the other Curates and decide on a plan of action." Anesko frowned and turned his attention from the wild dragons to me. "They look malnourished."

I nodded. "It's a long story."

"Walk with me. I want to know everything."

5

Master Anesko stood at the end of the table in the assembly room. He looked tired, and a myriad of red lines filled the whites of his eyes. Despite his obvious exhaustion, his demeanor was full of confidence, though I assumed it was a façade. I did not envy his position.

Maren sat on my left, and Katori was on my right. I finally felt at home again, but the feeling was tainted. I also knew the Citadel might not be our home much longer, depending on how things went. Anesko clasped his hands behind his back and cleared his throat, pulling me from my reverie.

"I think we all know how dire our situation is. We are, quite literally, surrounded by enemies, and their numbers are greater than our own."

An uneasy murmur echoed throughout the chamber. Anesko raised a hand for silence.

"What of the wild dragons?" Curate Henrik asked. "They should bolster our numbers."

"They are helpful, but we don't have enough riders for them. And judging by what I saw, they are not trained to fight. I fear many more of them will fall before this is over."

"If I may?" I said, standing up.

Anesko nodded.

"These dragons have been through a lot, and

they chose to come here to help us. But they do not plan on staying after this fight is over. They will leave and find a place to call their own. I know that is not what any of us wanted to hear, but I felt it prudent to mention before we decide on any course of action."

"Thank you, Eldwin," Anesko said. "With that in mind, it begs a question each of us must answer. If we turn the tides in our favor, what does the future hold?"

A sinking feeling tugged at my stomach, and I took my seat. Was he considering disbanding the riders again? That would be foolish, especially if we defeated the king's army. There would be a void of power, and the riders would need to fill it.

"Is the future of the Order in question? Again?" It was Henrik, and it was almost as if he was speaking my thoughts. Perhaps everyone in the room had the same fear.

"I am only asking a question, my friend. If we win this war, what happens? Osnen will need a new ruler, not only to guide her, but to protect her. Look around this room. We are all that is left of the leadership. The Terranese school is gone, and we have heard nothing from Valgaard since the Assembly imprisoned Hrodin. We are short of both riders and dragons. We must look ourselves in the mirror and admit the Order is dying."

His words cut me to my very core, and they stung as sharp as any wound because they were true. I looked at Maren. Her eyes were watery with tears. I grabbed her hand, and she squeezed mine in response. As much as I wanted to disagree with Anesko, I knew he was right. The Order *was* dying, and there didn't seem to be any way to stop it.

"If there is no hope, then why fight at all?" I asked. "Why not let the shield down and open the gates?" My question was sincere, but the words spilled out of my mouth with anger and pain.

"I am not saying that we should surrender, to the king or to fate," Anesko replied gently. "I only want us all to be aware of the reality that faces us."

I ground my teeth in frustration. All of us knew the reality, but no one was trying to change it.

"We know there are many difficulties ahead, but that has never stopped us before. Instead of focusing on the problems, we should turn our attention to finding solutions. Let's deal with the problem at hand. We are prisoners here so long as the king is at our gates. How do we drive him back? If you have an idea, no matter how outlandish, speak it now."

"We could retreat to the Terranese school," Katori said. "The king would have to march his army far indeed to reach those gates. By the time they arrived, we would hold every advantage."

"I don't think that's wise," Anesko replied. "Other than yourself, none of us are familiar with those grounds. We'd be at a disadvantage, just as the king would. Besides, we would still have to figure out a way to escape without notice."

"We could call on the Assembly," I suggested.

"How would they help?"

I paused, as I didn't have an appropriate answer. They were also busy with the dragon slayers and trying to find Risod.

"I … don't know," I said lamely.

Anesko looked around the table at each of us, but no other ideas were forthcoming. I leaned back in my seat and tried not to let the despair win. Maren and I had returned only to face our doom. Perhaps we should have stayed away from the Citadel and instead taken the wild dragons to a new home and started a new order.

*Do not think of such things.* Sion's voice lanced through my dark thoughts, scattering them.

*I'm sorry. I didn't mean for them to overwhelm me like that.*

A flood of comfort funneled through the bond, and despair was replaced with hope.

"My father will not stop until he has crushed the Order from existence," Maren said. "If we flee, he will follow us. We cannot run from this war. No, we must meet it head-on. We must strike him a direct blow."

Anesko turned his gaze to her. "How do you propose we do that? The lines of men between us and him are thick. Even if we were equal in number, the clash of arms would ruin both of our forces."

"We don't need to clash with his army to win.

We just need to cut the head from the snake. If my father falls, chaos will consume the others. His generals will fight one another for power, giving us the perfect distraction to finish them off or force them to surrender."

"We tried that already," I said. "We reached his tent and his sorcerers protected him."

"That is because they saw us coming."

"What are you thinking?" Anesko asked. "That we should cloak our movements?"

Maren shook her head. "No. Even if we could generate enough magic to hide our forces, his sorcerers would sense our spells before we could get close enough to do anything. What I propose is something else."

She paused for a moment, and I stared at her intently, wondering what she had come up with.

"We should send someone to kill him."

"An assassin?" Anesko asked. "We are warriors, not killers."

"In this case, we must be both. The one who goes will need to do so alone and without magic. What better way to hide than in plain sight?"

That was so simple, and yet so brilliant. And I knew immediately that it should be me. This had all started because the king wanted me, and that meant it would have to end with me.

"Under normal circumstances, I would never agree with such measures." Anesko sighed and rubbed his eyes. "But the situation we find ourselves in is far from normal. Whoever accepts this task may not be successful, and knowing the king, he will kill the one who fails. I do not think we should leave this to just any rider. It should be one of us in this room."

I nodded in agreement.

"Who will volunteer to kill the king?"

Before I could answer, Maren rose from her chair.

"There is no need for anyone to volunteer. I will do it."

# 6

"You cannot do this," I said.

"I should be the one to do it. He is my father, after all."

Anesko had dismissed the others and left, leaving Maren and me alone at the table.

"How will you get through the camp if you don't plan on using your magic?"

"I will disguise myself as one of his soldiers," she said simply.

"What if you get caught?"

"What if I don't?"

I knew arguing with her was pointless, but I couldn't let her risk her life. She would feel the same way if I went, so ultimately there was no way either of us could win this debate.

"I fear losing you," I whispered.

Maren slid her chair closer and leaned against me. I embraced her tightly.

"I'll be as safe as I can. I will kill him and come straight back here."

I had learned long ago there was no talking her out of something once she'd made up her mind, and I didn't plan on arguing with her anymore. No, instead, I would have to find a way to keep her from leaving the Citadel.

"You should probably go when it's dark," I said. "Are you going to tell Demris?"

"No. Please don't let Sion say anything to him."

I nodded. Maren smiled and planted a kiss on my lips, then stood up.

"Make sure you're part of the distraction Anesko has in mind, just in case something happens."

"I'll be there."

Maren left the room, and I stared at the wall absently, mulling over how I could get her to stay. Aside from forcefully locking her up, I couldn't think of anything.

*There is another way,* Sion's voice interrupted my thoughts. *Though Maren will be angry with you if you employ it.*

*What is it?*

*You could put her to sleep.*

*What do you mean?*

Sion sent an image through the bond of a toothed silver-green stalk that bore a white flower. I'd never seen it before.

*What is it?*

*It's a flower that can make a powder that causes drowsiness.*

*You want me to drug her?* It surprised me Sion

would even propose something like that.

*I was only offering a suggestion to your dilemma, though I dislike the idea of you going to the camp alone.*

*It's not like you can go with me, and I don't want Maren being taken captive or killed by her father.*

Sion rumbled, frustrated, but she had nothing else to say. I scratched an itch on my scalp and considered Sion's idea. She was right. Maren would be furious with me if I drugged her.

And yet …

It would keep her safe in the Citadel. It was that or temporarily lock her in the dungeon. Neither option was ideal, but I felt as though the flower was the least of two evils. I left the chamber and traversed the halls. A Curate that died during Hrodin's treachery had tended a small garden, and I figured that would be the best place to check for the flower considering Surrel from the library had taken it over.

The door to the botanical room was propped open, and I saw Surrel was inside. She held a watering can and was pouring water into a large pot of yellow flowers. I knocked on the door frame and she looked up.

"Son of Matthias," she greeted.

I smiled at her. She was one of the first people I met when I arrived at the school, and she had always been kind to me.

"Hello, Surrel. I need something, and I thought you might be able to help."

"Of course."

"I'm looking for a certain plant. It grows a white flower."

A glance around the room revealed that wasn't the best description since there was a multitude of white flowers. Clematis, periwinkle, hyacinth, rhododendron, and a few others I didn't know the name of were scattered in pots all over the room.

"Do you know the name of this flower?" she asked.

"Uh, I don't." Sion sent me the image of it again. "It secretes a milky fluid when the seed pod is cut. Does that help?"

"Yes, that narrows it down precisely. I have to ask, what do you need it for? That milky substance is known to be addictive for those who abuse its use."

"I can't say, unfortunately," I replied. "Master Anesko and …" I waved a hand around, indicating the school.

"Ah, yes. For our enemies. I understand."

Surrel set the watering can down and walked over to a pot of flowers that sat atop a shelf in the back corner of the room. She unsheathed a small blade from her waist and went to work, drawing the milky fluid out of the seed pods.

"How do the plants grow in here with no

sunlight?" I asked.

Surrel paused in her work to point at the globes of light that floated near the ceiling.

"Those were specifically designed to provide a light source as close to the sun as possible. They get the job done well, as you can see. How much of this stuff do you need?"

"Not much. Enough for one person should be sufficient."

She turned around and held out a glass vial. A small amount of thin pearly liquid sat at the bottom.

"You'll need to let it air dry, then crush it into a powder."

"Does it dissolve in water?"

"Yes, but I would suggest wine or tea, otherwise the taste is noticeable."

I took the vial and nodded.

"Thank you. As always, I appreciate your help."

"It is my pleasure, Son of Matthias."

"You know you can call me Eldwin," I said.

"I know." Surrel smiled and retrieved her watering can and resumed watering the flowers.

I clutched the vial in my hand and left. Maren didn't drink wine, so I would have to use tea to mask the powder. I went to our chambers and left the vial on the windowsill to allow the liquid to dry. Doubt tried to creep into my mind, but I ignored it. Maren would be angry, yes, but she would understand. At least, I hoped she would.

The rest of the day passed quickly, and by the time I returned to the room at dusk, the liquid had dried. I crushed the stuff into powder and hid the vial in my coin purse. At dinner, Maren and I sat at our usual table. My palms were sweating, and I had the feeling I was betraying her somehow.

I reminded myself why I was doing this. When Maren left the table for a moment, I poured the powder into her cup and quickly stirred it. She came back and took a drink. I prayed she wouldn't notice the taste. If she did, she said nothing.

The stuff must have been potent indeed, because it didn't take long for Maren to feel the effects of it. She moved sluggishly, and there were long pauses between her words.

"Are you feeling all right?" I asked.

"I'm not … sure."

She stared off at nothing, but her facial expression made it seem like she was seeing something interesting.

"Maybe you should go to bed."

"That … sounds great," Maren replied. "Wait. No. No, I can't. I have … something important to do, but … I can't remember what it is."

"I'm sure it'll come to you. Come on, I'll help you to bed. Some rest will do you some good."

She was unsteady on her feet and disoriented, and I again felt guilty for using the powder on her. I got her to our room and into the bed, and she passed out almost immediately.

*It's done,* I told Sion. *Now it's time to kill a king.*

# 7

I joined Anesko on the parapet of the wall and stared down at the camp that stretched out in front of the Citadel.

"Where's Maren?"

The question was innocent, but it made me feel as though Anesko knew what I had done. I swallowed the lump in my throat.

"Change of plans," I said. "She's not feeling well and laid down to rest. I'm going instead."

Anesko gave me a questioning look, but nodded.

"Very well."

"Have you decided what the distraction will be?"

"It is too dangerous to send anyone outside the walls, so unless you are in trouble, there will not be one."

I creased my brow in concern.

"Are you sure that's the best idea?" I asked. "With the focus elsewhere, it will be easier for me to sneak through the camp."

"I am sure. We would have to bring the shield down to send riders out, opening ourselves up to an attack. The risk is too great, especially with the king's riders so close to the walls."

"I'm on my own, then?"

"Not quite," Anesko said. "If you get into trouble, use this."

He held up a war horn. I took it and turned it over in my hands, inspecting it. It was carved of wood and had runes engraved on the sides. Wrapped around the wider end of it was a leather thong.

"So I blow into this, and what happens?"

"It will alert me, but those around you will hear nothing. Only use it if you are in grave danger. I don't want to risk our safety for the sake of anything less than your possible death."

I slipped the thong onto my belt and adjusted the horn so it rested against my right hip. My sword was sheathed on the left side, and the combined weight tugged at my pants in an unbalanced manner.

"If you can't bring the shield down, how do I get out there?" I asked.

"I will open a small hole in the barrier. You'll have to be quick, though. It won't stay open long, and if it closes on you, it'll kill you."

"Of course it will. If something happens and I don't make it back, tell Maren I'm sorry."

"For what?"

"She'll know," I replied, casting another look at the camp. There was no reason to delay the inevitable. "I'm ready if you are."

Anesko nodded. "Come with me."

He led the way down the stairs to the courtyard, then followed the wall around to the eastern end of the Citadel.

"Where are we going?"

"To a secret door. It is rarely used and is only for emergencies, so do not reveal it to anyone else."

Anesko paused at a portion of the wall that didn't have any torches. He placed a hand on the stones and felt around.

"You don't know how to open it?" I asked.

"I do, but as I said, it is rarely used. Ah, yes, here it is."

He pushed one stone with both hands and it sank into the wall with a soft scraping sound. There was a moment of silence, and then a two-foot by three-foot section of the wall slid back a few inches before disappearing into the stones on the right.

"That's not a very big door," I said.

"You'll have to crawl through."

"I figured."

We stared at one another for a moment before Anesko laid a hand on my shoulder.

"Be careful, Eldwin. I expect to see you back here before dawn."

"I'm always careful." He gave me a stern look, and I smiled sheepishly. "I always *try* to be careful."

"Don't try. Just do it."

"Yes, sir."

I knelt on the ground and waited. Anesko muttered some words, and the barrier faded from the open section of the wall. I hastily crawled through the makeshift doorway, then stood and brushed my hands off on my pants. I turned to look at the doorway and saw the barrier was already whole again. The stones slid back into place, closing me off from the Citadel. That part was easy enough.

*Do not get caught,* Sion said.

*I don't plan to.*

*We shall see.*

Clouds filled the night sky, leaving little light to see by, but it was the perfect cover for me to make my way into the camp. I stepped lightly and kept my hand on the hilt of my blade, mostly to keep it from swinging about. As I drew close to the border of the camp, I could see it was heavily guarded, with a constant stream of soldiers patrolling the perimeter.

The glow of campfires illuminated the outline of tents and other structures, and I skulked ahead quietly. Getting past the patrols was going to pose a challenge, but I had an idea. I waited until a group of soldiers marched past, then I sprinted to the nearest tent and squatted down, keeping to the shadows.

My heart was hammering in my chest, but it was

only partially from running. I was scared. No, terrified.

*Calm yourself,* Sion bade gently. *Stay alert.*

I nodded to myself, then took a few deep breaths. The footsteps of the next patrol drew close, and as they trudged past the opposite side of the tent, I stepped out from the shadows and joined them, walking at the rear of the group. None of them noticed me. I marched along with them until I spotted a row of tents that were backed up close to one another, providing an improvised path free from prying eyes.

I glanced over my shoulder and saw the next patrol was far enough away that they hopefully wouldn't see me break away. I counted silently in my head, and as we marched past the tents, I stepped into the shadows and hurried down the row. Fortune was with me, and again, no one noticed anything. I paused to get my bearings and peered between a gap in the tents to find the king's pavilion.

*It's so much easier to find things from the sky,* I complained to Sion.

*Of course, it is. Are you having trouble?*

*A little. I'm not sure where to go.*

*Show me.*

I sent an image of my surroundings through the bond.

*You are on the northeast side of the camp. The*

*king is in the center, so you'll need to go southwest. Move diagonally through the camp.*

*What would I do without you?* I asked.

*Probably die.*

I snorted and couldn't help but smile. With a clear direction in mind, I made my way across the camp, pausing in the shadows and hiding behind tents when soldiers were nearby. Before long, I reached the king's pavilion. I crept along the backside and heard the faint sound of voices coming from within the tent. It was probably Erling and his advisors. I remained where I was and waited impatiently for their meeting to end, constantly checking my surroundings for soldiers.

After what felt like an hour, the voices faded. I waited a few moments more and carefully cut a slit in the tent with my sword. I would have climbed under, but the tent canvas was stretched too tight to lift the bottom. Peering inside, I saw Erling sitting in an elegant chair, his back to me. In front of the chair was a brazier that flickered with orange flames.

*This is it.*

I clenched my hand around the hilt of my blade and slipped into the tent, stepping lightly. A massive plush rug covered the ground, and it helped to mute my steps. A few strides brought me behind the chair, and I raised the blade above my head, ready to strike Erling a death blow. My muscles tensed, and just as I was about to bring my sword down on the king's skull, the surrounding air rippled and I was frozen in place.

# 8

"Eldwin."

Erling's condescending tone filled my ears. He rose from the chair and turned to face me. I still found it odd that such an ugly man had fathered someone as beautiful and kind as Maren. His bald head was oily, and the firelight highlighted it, making his scalp shine. In this light, the red-purplish bruise that ran the length of the left side of his face gave him a sinister appearance.

I strained my muscles, but I couldn't move at all. Erling watched my obvious struggle, and his lips curled in an amused sneer.

"Fight all you want, but you will not get free."

He moved around the chair to stand in front of me and stared into my eyes. I poured all the hatred I had for him into my gaze.

"You are a fool if you thought you could so easily assassinate me. I have eyes everywhere, and nothing gets past my notice. I find it surprising that Anesko sent you to do the deed. Was he too afraid to do it himself? No matter. I'm glad you're here."

Erling lifted his right arm into my view. In his hand, he held a dagger. He placed the tip of the blade against my neck.

"I could slit your throat with hardly an effort," he said.

*I'm trapped,* I told Sion. *There's some sort of spell keeping me from moving.*

*Can you see the one who cast the spell?*

I couldn't move my head, but my eyes roamed around the tent. Erling was the only one I could see, but that didn't mean a sorcerer, or several of them, wasn't hidden using magic.

*No, I only see the king.*

Erling applied pressure to the dagger, causing the tip to break my skin. Warm blood trickled down my neck.

"Lucky for you, I don't want you dead. Not yet, anyway."

He removed the dagger and stepped back, tossing the weapon aside. I wasn't ignorant. He was as sly as a serpent, which meant he wanted something from me. The secret way into the Citadel, most likely. He would be disappointed, then. I would reveal nothing.

Erling made a motion with his hand, an obvious command of some kind, and the spell released my mouth.

"What do you want?" I snarled.

"Many things, as do all men," he replied.

"What do you want from *me*?"

"Ah, now you've asked the right question. I want you to tell me where I can find the Assembly."

"What?"

"Surprised, are you? Did you think I wanted to know how you got out of the Citadel with the barrier still up? I know there are many ways in and out of that blasted place, but I don't care about that. The school will fall when I am ready. What I want first is the Assembly."

If my face wasn't frozen, I would have scowled. "What do you want with the Assembly? They'll never give you an audience with them."

Erling snorted. "I don't need an audience, boy. I'm going to kill them. With their deaths, and the fall of the Order, I will have complete control over Osnen. There will no longer be pockets of power that do not answer to me. This is *my* kingdom."

His words were like a physical blow. He didn't just want to get rid of the Order, he wanted to murder the eldest dragons in the land. Erling was even more wicked than I thought.

"I won't tell you anything."

"I thought you might say that, so I will make myself abundantly clear. If you do not tell me what I want to know, I will destroy everything you care about while I make you watch."

"You can't," I growled. "You'll never get past the barrier."

"*I* don't need to. As I said, I have eyes *everywhere*. Right now, Maren is asleep, yes? And with you out here, there is no one in the school watching over her. Well … no one you'd like to be watching her, anyway."

Erling motioned with his hand and a shadow detached itself from the tent wall. A moment later, the inky blackness faded, revealing a light-haired man in leather armor. He wore a sword strapped at his waist and had the brightest green eyes I had ever seen.

"Show him," Erling said.

The man held his left hand out, palm upward. With his right hand, he traced a circle over his left and flicked his fingers upward. An image appeared between his hands, flickering and distorted, but there was no mistaking what it showed: Maren lying in bed asleep. And standing in the background near the window was a figure holding an unsheathed blade.

"She sleeps heavily tonight," the king murmured.

I swallowed hard. If I hadn't drugged her, she would be able to defend herself.

"Before you think to alert your dragon, know that Maren will be dead before anyone can come to her aid."

"You would kill your own daughter?" I had no doubt that he would, but I hoped there was some small amount of love or mercy in his heart.

"My daughter is already dead. She died to me the day she relinquished her nobility. I have no qualms with killing what remains of her."

"You underestimate her," I said. "When she wakes, she will know she's not alone. Your soldier will be dead before he moves to strike her."

"I am certain she will, which is why you have a limited amount of time to decide on your course of action. If you do not tell me where the Assembly is, I will have him kill her now while you watch."

*Do not tell him anything,* Sion said. *I will get Master Anesko.*

*No! Not yet. Erling isn't lying. Maren will be dead before Anesko can do anything. Do nothing until I tell you to.*

*If you tell him where the Assembly is, your value is gone and he'll kill you. There is no winning in this situation.*

I knew Sion was right, but there had to be another way. The Assembly was searching for Risod, which meant they probably weren't at the Temple of the Bond. Erling would have to navigate the maze, which he wouldn't be able to do without my help. I could lead him around for a while, and by the time we reached it, he would realize the Assembly members weren't there. It would buy me enough time to come up with a plan.

"Tell him to do it," Erling ordered.

"No, wait! I'll tell you!"

*Don't fall into his trap, Eldwin!*

*I know I don't deserve it, but please trust me.*

*What are you going to do?*

*I'll figure it out as I go, but do not tell anyone what's happening. Please.*

I could feel Sion's hesitation in the bond, but she ultimately agreed.

"I can tell you where their temple is, but you won't be able to find it."

"Why not?" Erling demanded.

"Powerful enchantments protect it. Those who seek the temple with ill will wander the woods around it forever." I didn't know if that last part was true, but it didn't hurt to exaggerate. "You will need someone to lead you through the magical labyrinth."

"Let me guess. That person would be you."

"I've been there before and I know the way. Do not harm Maren and I will take you to the Assembly."

"If you try anything, I'll gut you like a fish," Erling threatened.

"You have my word."

"Your word means nothing to me, lowborn."

I didn't know what else I could offer him, but thankfully, he didn't require any further assurances.

"Take his sword."

The sorcerer did as commanded and removed my blade from my hands, then patted me down for other weapons. He left the war horn, however. Satisfied I was fully disarmed, the sorcerer released his spell. My previous momentum returned, and my hands swung down, slamming painfully against the top of the chair. I hissed in a breath.

"We leave tonight," Erling said to the sorcerer. "Bring the others, as well as anything else you need."

The sorcerer bowed and exited the tent, leaving me alone with Erling. The hate I had for him burned intensely, and I was tempted to attack him with my bare hands, but I knew there were likely other guards hidden in the tent. I would bide my time, and when the opportunity arose, I would strike with fury.

# 9

We left within the hour. I was forced to ride with the sorcerer, whose name I learned was Shadamar. From what I could gather, he was the leader of Erling's private guard. A sorcerer, of all things. Though the more I thought about it, the more it made sense. When there were weapons other than swords and arrows involved, someone skilled with magic would be the best option for protection.

We flew east on the back of a large green dragon whose bulk was so thick that it stretched the straps of the saddle taut and the seams looked as if they might come undone. Erling rode with two others on a blue dragon, one a soldier and the other a sorcerer. Two other dragons, both red, followed behind us, each carrying three guards.

Despite the obvious danger, I enjoyed soaring through the sky in the darkness. The cool evening air ruffled my clothes, and the stars twinkled above. I had a front-row seat to the beauty of the night sky. One thing I didn't like was the further we got from the Citadel, the weaker my bond became. I could still feel Sion's presence, but it was muted, and eventually, we couldn't even speak normally with one another. It was more of an exchange of emotions, much like when we first bonded.

It was a feeling I didn't enjoy.

Regardless, I still had the war horn at my side. If things went badly, I could always use it, though it would take some time for Anesko to reach me, depending on where I was. I resigned myself to star gazing and tried not to think about the man Erling had watching over Maren. It seemed Anesko had not rid our ranks of all the spies, as he believed.

As the time passed, I dozed in the saddle. Shadamar, on the other hand, remained fully alert. It was difficult to determine his age, but he seemed young to me. I wondered how he had gained the attention of the king, but I assumed it was his magical prowess. It was no easy feat to exert control over another person, and he had stopped my attack on the king with ease. I would need to keep an eye on him, as he posed the biggest threat.

I must have fallen asleep, because I jolted suddenly when my stomach lurched. The dragon was descending. I gripped the saddle horn as the dragon continued its descent and wondered briefly if Maren was awake. I prayed she wasn't. She was safer asleep for now. I leaned to the side and scanned the ground, but it was too dark to make out anything other than vague outlines.

"Have we arrived?" I asked loudly.

"Yes," Shadamar answered.

A few moments later, the dragon touched the ground, its immense legs absorbing the impact of its landing. The other dragons landed nearby, the flapping of their wings causing gusts of wind to stir up the area. Ahead, I could see the outlines of trees.

How had the time passed so quickly?

"Get down," Shadamar ordered.

I climbed out of the saddle and leaped to the ground, stretching my legs and rubbing my lower back. The king's soldiers also dismounted, and they grouped together. Erling strode over and looked at me.

"Are there any traps we need to worry about?"

I shook my head. "No, none that I'm aware of. The enchantments were affected when magic failed, but there is no danger here."

"Good. Lead the way, then." He glanced at Shadamar. "Stay with him."

I glanced at the sky. It was still dark, but I guessed there were only a couple of hours until dawn. The magical forest would provide its own confusion, but I decided I would lead the king aimlessly around for a while. The Assembly would know we were here, and I hoped they were smart enough to discern what was happening.

"This way," I said.

The woods were eerie in the daylight, and much more so in the dark. Nocturnal animals skittered around in the brush, and the hooting of owls filled the air. There were no obvious trails, not that I would have followed them, anyway. I guided Erling and the others in a circular path, keeping to the outskirts of the forest. None of them caught on, at least for a while.

We were still trudging along when the first rays of sunlight peeked over the horizon, painting the sky with a palette of vibrant reds, oranges, and pinks. The colors of the forest became visible as daylight spilled across the land, and the chirping of birds replaced the nighttime sounds. I frowned. Something wasn't right. The forest had always been quiet, unnervingly so, yet it sounded full of life.

"What is taking so long?" Erling demanded. "I'm certain we've come this way already. What are you up to?"

"Nothing," I replied. "As I said, this place has powerful enchantments on it. The Temple of the Bond isn't found, it finds you."

"That makes no sense. What do you feel, Shadamar?"

The sorcerer gazed around the forest. "He is telling the truth. Ancient magic permeates this place, but it is … distorted. I cannot tell one enchantment from another. I'm afraid we are at his mercy."

Erling glared at me. "No more games. Take us to the temple or Maren dies."

There was no way for him to know whether I was fooling with him, but I didn't want to press my luck. Maren was too important to me.

"Empty whatever is in your minds. The magic will not allow us entrance if it knows your intentions are ill."

Shadamar looked at the king. "Do as he says."

I waited a moment, then continued through the woods, subtly angling our direction toward the center of the forest. I knew we were on the right course when I began to see things that weren't there. From my periphery, I could see shadows among the trees whispering and pointing at us, but when I looked at them directly, they were gone.

*Yes,* I told myself. *This is the way.*

The exhaustion and drowsiness set in slowly, and I could see the concern growing on Shadamar's face.

"Don't worry," I said, my words slurring slightly. "This is normal. It's the work of … the work of … of the magic."

Erling was the first to collapse. Shadamar stopped but made no move to assist him. Neither did any of the others. They were all fighting the effects of the magic, but one by one, they all dropped to the forest floor. Shadamar was the last of Erling's men to do so. The last thing that rolled around in my mind before I fell face-first onto the leafy ground was surprise, surprise that I stayed conscious longer than the sorcerer.

# 10

When I opened my eyes, I was staring at Shadamar's boots.

I pushed myself up onto my hands and knees and looked straight. The black stones of the Temple of the Bond glinted under the sun. Nemryth was standing a few feet away, a scowl plastered on her face.

"Why did you lead them here?" she demanded.

"I'm sorry. I had no choice. You must leave. Now. The king seeks your destruction."

"We will not leave our home. If the king wants a fight, I will give him one."

"No." I shook my head. "He has a soldier watching Maren. If you kill the king, the soldier will kill her."

Nemryth stared at me for a long moment in silence.

"Fine," she said. "We're still searching for Risod, so that will give us an excuse to leave the temple. How long do you need?"

An idea came to me.

"Is there anything of Risod's you can give me?"

"Why?"

"The king wants to find you, but because of the

enchantments of the forest, he wasn't able to. He needed me to show him. I'm sure his sorcerer here," I kicked Shadamar's foot, "can track Risod down if he had one of her belongings. It's how someone found me once. He will lead us to the dragon slayers, and if all goes well, they'll wipe each other out."

Nemryth smirked, and I knew she liked my plan.

"That's clever of you," she said. "I will leave something out for them to find. Once they are on the trail, we will follow you."

"Don't let them see you or that will throw off everything."

"They will not detect our presence."

I nodded. "You should go before they wake up."

Nemryth chuckled. "You know we control when the magic lets you wake up, don't you? They will not come to until I let them. It is the only thing about the enchantments that has not changed."

I did not know that, but it was great news.

"Put me back to sleep," I said. "And let the king wake before me. This needs to be believable."

"As you wish. We will leave now. It won't take long. Hopefully, this works."

"It will," I said. It had to.

"See you soon."

The grogginess washed over me, and I crumpled

to the ground. The next thing I knew, someone was shaking my shoulder. I opened my eyes to see Erling standing over me. His guards were gathered around him, weapons drawn.

"Get up," Erling said.

I wasn't sure how long I had been down, but the sun wasn't much further into the sky. Rising to my feet, I glanced around the clearing.

"Where are they?"

I pointed at the temple. "They should be inside there."

"Take the lead," he ordered.

I walked across the clearing and ascended the steps. The king and his men followed at a distance. He was being wary. I pushed against the doors, but they didn't budge.

"It's locked," I said, looking over my shoulder.

Erling nodded his head at Shadamar. "Open them."

The sorcerer joined me near the doors and held his right hand up. He flicked his gaze at me. "Get behind me."

I did as he said. A bright light flashed into existence, temporarily blinding me. A moment later, the sound of splintering wood filled the air. When my vision came back, I saw Shadamar's spell had blasted the doors to pieces. He strode into the temple, a flickering red-orange ball of flame in his hand. Erling and the rest of his men streamed into the building, one of them pulling me forcefully along.

"Split up," the king said. "Search everywhere."

"You're with me," Shadamar said, motioning for me to follow him.

I figured if I did everything without question, it might be suspicious. I folded my arms across my chest.

"I'll stay here. This is your suicide mission, not mine."

One of the soldiers behind me kicked me in the back of my right knee, dropping me to the floor. I gritted my teeth against the pain and anger.

"The next order you ignore will cost you a limb," the man threatened.

I slowly climbed back to my feet and shot him a glare. The soldier was grinning like an idiot, clearly amused.

"Do as Shadamar says," Erling said. "He holds the power over Maren's life."

That reminder helped keep my focus on the plan. I followed Shadamar as he traversed the halls on the western side of the temple. We entered room after room, all of them empty. There were no beds or anything else, just cold rooms of stone.

"Maybe they knew you were coming," I said.

Shadamar whirled around, the ball of flame crackling inches from my face. "Did you warn them?"

"How would I? I'm not bonded to any of them."

The sorcerer gave me an intense stare before turning around and continuing his search. The last door at the end of the hall had a silver plaque with a red gem in it. It was a ruby. I assumed it was Risod's personal chambers. Shadamar pushed the door open, and we stepped inside. It was the first room that showed any signs of someone's presence. There was a neatly made bed, a side table with a lantern, and at the end of the bed was a large storage chest.

"Open the chest," Shadamar said.

I begrudgingly obeyed. There were some clothes at the bottom, but what caught my eye was an ornate dagger in a leather sheath. The pommel of the blade held a ruby that seemed to glow with a light of its own. I grabbed it and held it up.

"I found this."

"Hand it over."

I gave it to the sorcerer and glanced around the room as he studied the weapon. There was nothing else of interest.

"Can you use that to track them or something?" I asked, trying to sound helpful.

Shadamar stuffed the dagger into his belt and left the room. I hurried after him and we returned to the main chamber. The others were already there.

"There's no one here," Erling said. "If you led me on a wild goose chase, I'll—"

"This is the right place," Shadamar interrupted. "They may not be here now, but I can find them."

"How?"

"With this." Shadamar held up the dagger. "It has a magical connection to something else, something one of them has on their person. I can use it to find them."

I found it funny that the sorcerer took credit for my idea, but it didn't matter. As long as the king bought into it, that was all that mattered.

"Any idea where they would be?" Erling asked, looking at me.

"No. As far as I'm aware, they never leave this place."

Erling looked at Shadamar and nodded. The sorcerer closed his eyes and muttered words under his breath. The silence stretched on, and I worried the dagger might not have been the item Nemryth intended us to find. When Shadamar opened his eyes, a red glow emanated from his pupils.

"I can see the trail," he said. "We must go west."

Erling smiled, likely thinking he was on the verge of victory.

"Move out," he commanded. "Let's find these blasted dragons."

# 11

We flew west for several hours, Shadamar's spell guiding us. Little did he know, he was leading the king to his doom. I tried not to glance back too often, but the times I did, I saw no sign of the Assembly members. Either we had lost them, or they were doing an amazing job of hiding.

It was risky for me to be there when the king's men encountered the dragon slayers, but I figured it would give me the opportunity to slip away and escape. Given how my plans usually worked out, that likely wouldn't happen, but I could hope.

My thoughts strayed to what the dragon slayers were doing in Osnen. Nemryth thought they arrived on accident, and at first, I did, too … but now I wasn't so sure. Hunting dragons was what they did, but the fact they captured a member of the Assembly didn't seem to be a coincidence.

Morning turned to noon, and my stomach growled. I hadn't eaten since dinner the night before, and hunger was clawing at me. The king and his men had breakfast, but of course, they didn't share their food with me. With a minor amount of luck, I'd find something to eat after escaping.

The sun was in the middle of the sky, but the breeze that whipped around me as we flew made the heat unnoticeable. The landscape below gradually changed, and soon, I could see the city of Tiradale in the distance. Now I knew exactly where I was. The dragon we rode veered left of the city, heading in a southern direction.

"We're close," Shadamar shouted. "It isn't much farther."

I instinctively reached for my sword and then remembered the sorcerer had taken it from me. It was my father's blade, and I couldn't leave it behind. I didn't know where it was, either, and I cursed the man under my breath.

A thin line of smoke drifted into the sky, and I spotted the camp. It was nestled among a few small hills. Several tents were encircled around a cooking fire, but I didn't see any movement. The dragon began a slow circling descent and landed a fair distance from the camp. Erling's mount landed next, followed by the others. I climbed down and traced my fingers along the smooth wood of the war horn at my waist. I'd almost forgotten I had it.

"Why did we land here?" Erling asked as he strode to where Shadamar and I stood.

"He refuses to get closer," the sorcerer replied, motioning to the dragon. "He smells something he doesn't like."

Did the dragon slayers have some sort of deterrent? Or maybe the dragon could sense their enchanted weapons, designed specifically to kill his kind.

"Stubborn creatures. We go on foot, then. The dragons can provide support from the sky."

Shadamar was silent for a moment. "He refuses to get any closer."

Erling's face hardened, but there was little he could do. It was impossible to force a dragon's will.

"I didn't see anyone in the camp," Erling said, changing the subject. "They must be in the tents."

Shadamar nodded. "That was my thought as well. They don't know we're coming, so we have the advantage."

"There are five of them and ten of us. The numbers are doubled in our favor."

Shadamar frowned. "There are nine of us, my Lord. You should stay back with the prisoner to ensure your safety. We don't know what they are capable of, or if more have joined them."

"We are all going, including Eldwin." Erling drew his sword.

"As you say." Shadamar also unsheathed his blade, and I saw it was my sword.

"That's mine," I said.

"Not anymore." Shadamar smirked at me, and I wanted nothing more than to punch him in the face.

Without another word, Erling turned and marched toward the hills that surrounded the camp. Shadamar nodded for me to follow, and I trudged after the king. The rest of the soldiers walked behind us. The hills weren't too steep, and we swiftly crested them.

Below, I counted five tents. The material they

were made of looked like leather, but there was something strange about the patterns on them. Each one was unique, but there was nothing uniform about any of them. They were irregular and looked like …

My eyes widened. They made their tents of dragon hide. Revulsion overwhelmed me and I felt bile rise in my throat. I quickly swallowed to keep it down and looked at Erling. Either he didn't notice, or he didn't care. I was certain it was the latter.

"Two to a tent," Erling said. "Keep a close eye on Eldwin here. We don't need him running off."

Shadamar pressed the tip of his sword—*my sword*—into my back and prodded me painfully with it. I hesitantly scaled down the hill and reached the bottom without too much trouble. I was concerned that if Shadamar slipped and tumbled down, he'd accidentally impale me, but thankfully, he kept his balance.

Erling took a step forward, and Shadamar grabbed him by the arm, pulling him back. Erling's scowl caused the sorcerer to falter, but he cleared his throat.

"Forgive me, but we should send someone else ahead first."

"Is there a trap?"

"I don't sense anything, but not all traps are made of magic."

Erling grunted in reply and nodded his agreement. Shadamar looked at the other sorcerer, the one who rode with the king, and he pointed. He held a finger up to his lips, indicating he should be quiet. The man bowed his head and walked ahead stealthily. I watched him draw nearer to the camp and wondered why the dragon slayers hadn't made an appearance yet. Were they asleep in the middle of the day?

They couldn't all be, not if they held Risod captive. The man angled right, heading for the tent closest to him. His steps grew more confident the closer he got, and the other soldiers shuffled forward eagerly. The hairs on my arms stood on end, and as quickly as I blinked, the sorcerer crossed some sort of invisible line that set off a ward. An explosion shook the ground. I crouched down and shielded my face with my right arm.

Dust and debris showered the area, and the power of the blast tore a trench in the earth. The sorcerer's mutilated body lay in a heap twenty feet away from where he'd been. Everything was silent for a long moment. Erling and the others were clearly surprised, and before any of them could recover their wits, the dragon slayers rushed out from their tents.

Erling was the first to move. He rushed forward, clashing swords with a tall brute covered in tattooed markings. The other soldiers followed their king's example and engaged the enemy. I stumbled backward and looked up the hill. It was the perfect opportunity to escape, but that meant leaving my father's sword behind. It also meant risking Maren's life in the event the king and his men overpowered the slayers.

The battle was raging fiercely, and both sides seemed evenly matched. The clanging of swords reverberated through the air, and for a moment, I thought the king would be victorious. One of his soldiers fell, cut down by a man wielding an axe. I recognized him from my previous encounter with the slayers. He roared in triumph and cut down another soldier. Another slayer, a woman in chain mail, struck a mortal wound to the soldier beside Shadamar.

Half of Erling's men had fallen, and not a single slayer was dead or injured. I stared at Shadamar, cursing the man again for taking my father's sword. I chewed on my lower lip and decided to cut my losses. There was no way Erling was going to win this battle now. I started to climb the hill and looked back when I heard a scream of pain. The tattooed brute had driven his sword into Erling's leg.

*Good,* I thought. *Let him suffer and die.*

A thunderclap roared, the sound so loud I involuntarily cowered and lost my footing. I fell and rolled back down the hill. A blazing white light surrounded Shadamar, and it expanded outward, turning several dragon slayers into ash. I spotted Risod as she was dragged from one of the tents by a slayer who had not been part of the battle. The remaining slayers fled, and Shadamar dropped to his knees.

# 12

I scrambled onto my feet and ran to where Shadamar was, intending to take my sword from him. As I reached for it, I froze in place, just as I had in the king's tent. Apparently, Shadamar was not as exhausted as he appeared. He glared at me and rose to his feet, then strode past to where Erling was crying out in agony, leaving me unable to move.

After a long moment of screaming, Erling fell silent, and I wondered if he was dead. Shadamar released me from the spell and I turned to look. Erling was still lying on the ground, but Shadamar had tied off his leg to slow the bleeding.

"Help me carry him," the sorcerer said. "We need to get him to a healer."

I scoffed at the request. "I'd rather let him lie there and bleed to death."

Shadamar pointed the sword at me. "You will help me or Maren will die, and then I'll kill you."

Sion had offered to get help, and I'd told her not to. I regretted that now. While the distance wasn't as great between us, I still couldn't communicate with her. Her emotions came through the bond clearly, mostly curiosity, but I couldn't use emotions to instruct her what to do. Until we closed the distance further, I would have to continue to play the obedient prisoner.

With an exaggerated sigh, I walked over and knelt beside Erling. The wound in his leg was a gaping hole about two inches in diameter. Blood soaked his pants and stained the ground beneath him. I was no expert, but I didn't think he would survive long enough to reach a healer.

"We need to pull him up by his arms," Shadamar said. "I've done the best I could with his leg, but we'll need to be careful."

I glanced up the hill. Although it wasn't too steep, dragging a limp body up it would hardly be a simple task. Erling was lucky his sorcerer hadn't died like the rest of his men. There was something fitting about letting him bleed out all alone, but alas, we didn't always get what we wanted.

"Can't you just use your magic to fly him up there?" I asked.

"If I could, do you think I'd be asking for help to carry him? He is protected against magic."

A lot made sense with that information, though I wondered how that worked. Did he have some sort of talisman that negated magic near him, or was it something else?

"Quit gawking and help me," Shadamar demanded.

We each grabbed one of his arms and pulled him up. It was a challenge because he was deadweight, but also because Shadamar was trying to keep the king's injured leg from moving too much. Once we had his arms slung across our shoulders, we started the trek up the hill. The going was slow and precarious, but we eventually reached the top and Shadamar cursed.

The dragons were gone.

I scanned the sky, but there was no sign of them. They must have fled when the battle erupted. That, or the smell of the dragon hide tents was enough to keep them from sticking around. I didn't blame them for leaving, but it was a major inconvenience. We stood there for a long moment, and I assumed Shadamar was trying to decide what to do.

"I'm surprised your dragon abandoned you," I said, side-eyeing him.

"I am not bonded to a dragon," he replied.

"Why not?"

"It is a weakness I do not need."

He couldn't have been more wrong. Being bonded to a dragon was not a weakness, but a strength.

"You know as well as I do he will not make it, even if the dragons were still here."

"You better hope not. If the king dies, so does Maren."

"Why do you serve him?" I asked, growing aggravated. "He's a tyrant."

"Do not concern yourself with that," Shadamar said. "We have to get him to Tiradale."

"How do you expect to do that? We have no

way to transport him."

"I will make a stretcher."

"And do what? Carry him the entire way? Tiradale is miles from here."

"Yes," Shadamar said. "We will carry him. Here, set him down."

We laid Erling down on the ground. He groaned softly, but remained unconscious.

"Stay here. If you try to run, you won't get far."

Shadamar went back down the hill to the camp. I turned my gaze east and searched the sky for the Assembly, but I still didn't see them. Where were they? Why hadn't they arrived yet? Since there was nothing else to do but wait, I sat on the ground beside the king. His breathing was shallow and his skin was pale.

I looked down at the camp and watched Shadamar as he worked. He cut a portion of dragon hide from one of the tents, then chopped one of the tent poles in half and attached the hide to the pieces. His hands glowed as he ran them along the poles, fusing the material to the wooden shafts. When he finished, he had a makeshift litter. Shadamar carried it up the hill and set it down next to Erling.

"Grab his legs and lift as gently as you can."

I reluctantly did so, scrunching my face in disgust when my hand touched warm blood. Shadamar was going above and beyond what I would expect for a man who was certainly dying.

Why was he so loyal to Erling? What had the king promised him? I didn't bother to ask, since I knew the man would tell me nothing.

We set Erling on the litter and I knelt and brushed my hand against the ground, trying to remove the blood. My head snapped to look at Erling as a loud gasp escaped him. His eyes fluttered open.

"Easy, my Lord," Shadamar said. "Don't move. You are injured, but I will get you somewhere safe."

I doubted the king was coherent enough to understand him, but he turned his head to the side to look at the sorcerer.

"Assembly?" he wheezed.

Shadamar shook his head, casting a baleful look in my direction. "They were not here. We need to leave before the slayers return."

"I'm not going anywhere with you," I said. "Not unless you guarantee Maren's safety and call off your war against the Order."

"You have nothing to bargain with!" Shadamar snapped.

"Without my help, the king will bleed to death. It seems we are at an impasse."

"I will do it," Erling said weakly.

"My Lord?"

"If he will help, I will do as … as he asks." Erling's face tensed with pain and he fell back into unconsciousness, his head lolling to the side awkwardly.

I was no fool. The king was lying to get what he wanted. A small part of me hoped he would realize his folly, but that depended on him surviving, which didn't seem likely to me.

"Are you satisfied?" Shadamar asked.

Of course, I wasn't, but the alternative was too risky. Once we reached Tiradale, I'd be close enough to communicate with Sion. She could inform Anesko about what was happening, and I was confident he could deal with the soldier watching over Maren. With her safety guaranteed, I would be free to finish off the king. The only thing that stood in my way was Shadamar.

I needed to get rid of him.

# 13

I found some food in the camp and devoured it, partially because I was ravenously hungry and partially because Shadamar rushed me at sword point. With a full stomach, I felt more energized. Shadamar forced me to walk at the front of the litter, which I assumed was because he wanted to keep his eyes on me.

We walked for hours before Shadamar allowed for a brief break beside a slow-moving stream. I drank my fill and soaked my hands in the cool water, easing the discomfort. Several blisters had formed on my palms from the friction of holding the tent poles for so long, and my arm muscles throbbed with soreness.

"Let's get back to it," Shadamar said.

I sighed and rose to my feet, waving my hands back and forth to fling the water from them. Erling remained unconscious, but his bleeding had stopped. His chest moved up and down with his feeble breath. I thought about telling the sorcerer that we were toiling in vain, but I was too tired to argue with him.

We picked up the litter and continued until dusk descended over the land and the city of Tiradale came into view. It surprised me at how quickly we covered the distance and assumed I must have over-judged how far from the city we had been.

At the gates, Shadamar informed the city guards of what had transpired and one of them rushed off to notify the baron. It seemed like ages since I had last been in Tiradale, but the city had changed little. The streets bustled with activity, and upbeat music from a nearby tavern drifted into the air.

It wasn't long before more guards arrived. They took over carrying the litter, for which I was thankful, but then they escorted us through the city to the castle. When Maren and I had come here to investigate the missing children, we'd entered the castle grounds through the side gate. The crowds parted to make way for us, and the soldiers led us straight through the main entrance.

Baron Giffor and a retinue of servants were waiting in the courtyard. Healers in white robes immediately inundated the soldiers carrying the litter. I watched wordlessly, surprised that the baron's loyalty didn't waver with the king in such a vulnerable state.

"My lord," Shadamar greeted, offering a tired bow. "I apologize for intruding on you, but your city was the closest that could help."

Giffor waved his words away. "Nonsense. It's the least I can do for the king."

Realization struck me suddenly that the baron might be thinking of how he could benefit from helping Erling. Perhaps there was more reward for him in doing that than trying to usurp the throne. Court politics were far from my realm of knowledge. With everyone's attention on the king, it would be easier to slip away unnoticed.

"Take him to the infirmary," Giffor ordered.

The soldiers holding the litter marched off, and Shadamar started to go with them.

"He's in excellent hands," the baron said.

"I do not doubt the talents of your people, my lord. It is my duty to keep watch over the king at all times."

"A man of loyalty. I respect that. If it makes you feel more at ease, we can walk with them."

"Please," Shadamar said.

*Now is my chance,* I thought.

"This one is a prisoner of the king," the sorcerer added, looking at me.

Giffor turned his attention in my direction, and his eyes widened in shock. "El ... Elfin?"

"Eldwin," I corrected.

"Ah, yes. You managed to get into trouble with the king, did you? Not a wise move."

"The king is a tyrant," I spat. "And his accusations are baseless."

The baron exchanged looks with Shadamar.

"He stays with me," the sorcerer said.

"Very well." He motioned to one of his guards and the man came to stand beside me. "Keep an eye on him."

We followed the litter into the castle and I listened to the two of them talk.

"As soon as your healers have done their work, we need to get the king back to the Citadel. Are there any riders here that can take us?"

"I'm afraid not," Giffor said. "They were all withdrawn to the Citadel, per the king's request. He can stay here as long as necessary."

"You are too kind, but there are matters that still need to be dealt with that require his presence there."

Shadamar glanced back at me and leaned in close to the baron, lowering his voice so that I couldn't make out what he said. I didn't have to hear his words to know what it was about. The king was a snake, and he would never keep his word about ending his war. I reached out through the bond.

*Sion? Can you hear me?*

*I can. Where are you?*

Her presence within my mind was a wave of comfort, and I relished the feeling.

*I'm in Tiradale. The king was attacked by the dragon slayers, and I'm being held prisoner.*

*I am coming to you. I will raze the city if they harm you.*

*No, stay at the Citadel. I need you to deliver a message to Anesko.*

*What is it?*

*There is a soldier there that the king employs. He's watching Maren and plans to kill her if I don't do whatever the king wants. Anesko needs to find him.*

*I will tell him,* Sion said. *And then I am coming to get you.*

*Do not risk your safety for mine. Anesko will not lower the barrier for you unless it is a matter of life or death. I am safe for now. If that changes, I will tell you.*

Sion rumbled through the bond, her aggravation evident.

*Besides, I'm waiting for an opportunity to kill the king. He's tougher than I thought, and now that he's with Baron Giffor's healers, he's probably going to pull through his injury. I just have to figure out how to get his sorcerer to leave his side.*

*Kill him, too.*

*Were it so easy, I'd have already done so. He's as powerful as Maren, if not more so.*

*I will ask Anesko if there is anyone in Tiradale loyal to the Order,* she said. *Perhaps we have allies there who can help.*

*I doubt it, but it doesn't hurt to ask.*

We turned down a wide hall, and they carried the king into a chamber that looked similar to the infirmary at the Citadel. The soldiers set the litter down on the floor and stepped aside, allowing the healers to take over. They gently lifted him onto a cot and continued their work. Giffor dismissed all the soldiers except the one keeping watch over me and turned his attention back to Shadamar.

"I can give you horses," he said. "They are fast, but I don't foresee the king being able to ride any time soon."

Shadamar's brow creased. "We will see how he is doing in the morning. He may surprise us."

"He may indeed." Giffor flicked his gaze to me. "What of him?"

"Lock him in the dungeon."

# 14

My cell didn't feel like it was in the dungeon. It was clean and well-lit. There were a few other prisoners, but they were on the farther end of the corridor. A small cot was in the corner, but considering they chained me to the wall, I couldn't reach it, so I sat on the floor with my back pressed against the cold stone wall.

The guard on duty gave me a hunk of bread. It wasn't much, nor was it fresh, but it filled my stomach and sated my hunger. Eventually, the guard walked down the corridor, extinguishing the lanterns. Left in the dark with only my thoughts, and utterly exhausted, I leaned my head back and stared at the shadows above me.

It was impossible to judge the passage of time, and I closed my eyes to rest them for a moment. The clank of the cell door woke me, and I squinted against the glow of a lantern. Was it morning already? My eyes slowly adjusted, and I sat up. The chill in the cell had grown, and I rubbed my arms.

"What is it?" I asked.

"Eldwin. Are you hurt?"

I knew that voice. I stared at the figure holding the lantern until the details of her face became clear.

"Master Katori? What are you doing here?"

"I've come to rescue you."

She placed the lantern on a hook on the wall, then knelt and unlocked my shackles with an iron key attached to a thick ring. I flexed my wrists and stood up.

"Is Maren safe?"

"Yes," Katori replied. "Anesko got the message you gave Sion. We have dealt with the spy."

"Dealt with?"

"He was executed."

Relief washed over me. "That's great."

"Death is never something to be applauded," she said.

"No, that's not what I meant. I'm just glad she's out of harm's way. Are you the only one here?"

"Yes. Anesko did not want to risk lowering the barrier to let Sion out, so I left the same way you did."

I nodded. Now that Maren was safe, I could leave and there was nothing Shadamar or Erling could do about it. Erling.

"I know where the king is," I said.

"What do you mean?"

"I left the Citadel to kill him. Things didn't go as planned, and the dragon slayers injured him. He's in the infirmary."

"I'm sure the baron has guards watching over him."

"Maybe, but I'm not worried about them. It's Shadamar I'm worried about."

"Who is Shadamar?"

"The king's personal guard. He's a sorcerer, so I will need your help."

"Anesko told me to get you out of here and return to the Citadel. We should go before someone sees us."

I shook my head. "I can't go back, not until the king is dead. We have the chance to end this war here and now. I can't do it without you."

Katori heaved a resigned sigh. "Very well. Lead the way."

I smiled and hurried out of the cell. The way here had been easy to memorize, and I backtracked the way the guards had brought me. We didn't encounter any soldiers along the way, but we kept to the shadows when possible and slipped through the castle halls as quietly as we could. Once we reached the chamber that led to the infirmary hall, I paused.

Two guards were standing at the entrance to the hall. They were talking, clearly not expecting any trouble. While they wore swords strapped at their waists, they weren't wearing proper armor.

"We need to get rid of them," I whispered.

"I'll put them to sleep."

"No. If you use magic, Shadamar might sense it."

"What do you propose, then?"

I looked around the chamber, and my gaze landed on a metal sconce on the wall.

"I have an idea. Follow me."

Taking the sconce off the wall, I carried it out in front of me and approached the guards. They stopped talking and moved to block the way ahead.

"This way is off limits," one of them said.

"Apologies, sir. A prisoner escaped, and the captain sent us to ensure he didn't go after the king."

The guards exchanged looks, which was the opening I needed. I swung the sconce into the side of one guard's head. A sickening crack echoed off the walls, and the man collapsed on the floor. The other guard stumbled backward into the hall, drawing his sword. I rushed forward, waving the sconce back and forth wildly.

The soldier brought his blade up and it clanged against the sconce. The sound reverberating along the hall. I cursed, hoping it didn't alert Shadamar or any other guards. Katori pushed past me and drove her fist into the guard's side. He grunted and tried to back up further, but we closed in on him. I jabbed the pointed end of the sconce at him while Katori dropped low and swept his legs out from under him. He landed on his rear end and Katori followed through with a knee to his head, knocking him unconscious.

"We need to hurry," she huffed. "The noise will

surely have caught someone's attention."

"This way."

I led her to the infirmary and peered around the doorway. Erling was still lying in the same bed, and Shadamar was sleeping in chair beside him. No other guards were present. That seemed foolish to me, but then again, there was no reason to believe the king would be in danger within the baron's walls.

"There," I whispered, pointing. "That's the sorcerer."

"I will deal with him."

I entered the room and saw my sword lying on the floor at Shadamar's feet, within easy range if he needed it. Stepping quietly, I retrieved it and stared at the sorcerer, wondering again why he was so loyal to Erling. I nodded at Katori and unsheathed the blade, gently poking Shadamar in the chest with it. His eyes cracked open, and it took him a moment to realize what was happening. He moved to rise from the chair, but before he could, Katori finished uttering the words to a spell that froze him in place, much like he had done to me in Erling's pavilion.

"Sleeping on the job? That's a shame. Do you remember how you threatened to kill my wife? To kill me?"

I pressed the tip of my sword against Erling's ribcage. Shadamar's eyes filled with rage, but he could do nothing.

"Erling's reign of tyranny is over. I want you to

see him die so that you suffer, knowing that you were powerless to save him. You don't like the feeling, do you? I imagine not. Now you know how it feels."

I held Shadamar's gaze and steeled myself for what needed to be done. For all my talk, it was no easy task to take another person's life. I reminded myself of the terrible things Erling had said to me, the way he treated the people of the kingdom that he viewed as beneath him. All of it helped fuel my anger, and with one swift move, I forced my sword through Erling's side and into his heart.

He made a noise in his throat. I stood still, hardly believing I actually did it. The king was dead by my hand. I twisted the hilt, opening the wound further, then jerked my blade free. Blood poured from the wound, staining the bed and running off onto the floor. I looked at Katori.

"It is done," she hissed. "Let us go."

I wiped the blood off my sword using Erling's body, then sheathed the weapon and strapped it to the belt around my waist. Shadamar's eyes were watery with tears, but the rage in his gaze only intensified.

"Never forget this act," I told him.

Katori and I left the room, and a part of me died with the king.

# 15

We returned to the Citadel on the winds of magic, thanks to Katori. She transported us to the hidden door outside the walls. It was still dark, but I assumed dawn would arrive soon.

"Tell Sion we've returned."

I reached through the bond and touched Sion's mind. She was sleeping, but sensing my presence, she quickly awoke.

*Katori and I are here,* I said.

The bond flooded with her enthusiasm. It was infectious, and I couldn't stop smiling despite my feelings toward what I'd done. That, and although I'd only been away a few days, not being able to speak with her had been more miserable than I realized.

*I will inform Master Anesko.*

We waited in silence, not even daring to risk whispering to one another for fear someone would hear us. I kept my eyes to the south and watched the flicking firelights of the enemy encampment. After a few moments, which felt longer because of my impatience, the hidden door in the wall slid open. I knelt and looked through. Anesko was there, along with Curate Henrik and Maren.

"You first," I said, looking up at Katori.

She dropped onto her hand and knees and

crawled through. The barrier returned, sizzling the disrupted dirt. I watched Anesko and waited. As soon as the barrier came down again, I hurried across the threshold.

"Eldwin!"

Maren embraced me before I was fully back on my feet, and we tumbled to the ground. She kissed me fiercely, and I returned it with equal passion.

"I'm sorry," I whispered, flicking my gaze at the others. "I shouldn't have—"

"I'm not mad at you, Eldwin. I mean, I was at first, but I'm just glad you're all right."

Anesko stepped close and cleared his throat. "I hate to intrude on your private moment, but I must know. Were you successful?"

I looked from Maren to Anesko and back.

"Yes. The king is dead."

Maren gave a slight nod, her expression giving no hint of her emotions. Her eyes, however, told another story. It was like looking into a mirror and seeing my inner turmoil on display.

"Then it is over," Anesko said. It could have been my imagination, but it seemed as though an invisible weight lifted from him, and his shoulders rose.

"It was in the baron's castle in Tiradale," I added. "Only one of his sorcerers knows. He was the only one who survived with us."

"The news won't reach his camp until morning,

I'm sure. You've done us a great service, Eldwin."

I knew his words were true, but they rang hollow. "I only did what any of us would have done."

"You strode into great danger at the behest of others. Few would willingly do so. Sunrise will be upon us soon. Let us try to get some rest. Who knows what awaits us when the news arrives."

Maren climbed off me and helped me to my feet. I brushed my backside off and the five of us walked together through the courtyard. Aside from a few guards on the walls, there was no one else out at this hour. Our footsteps were the only noise. They sounded so loud echoing off the stone walls.

We entered the school and before everyone parted ways, Anesko said, "Come see me in the morning. I want to know everything."

"We can meet now if you'd prefer. There's something I need to speak with you about, anyway."

"Surely it can wait until the morning? I am weary to the bone."

We needed to take a group of riders out to find the Assembly and deal with the dragon slayers, but I knew that until the army camped outside the walls was gone, Anesko would not consider lowering the barrier.

"It can wait," I said.

He offered a tired smile in thanks and strode off down the hall. Maren wrapped her right arm around my left and we headed for our room.

"I'm sorry," I told her again.

"It's fine."

"No, it isn't. I …" Would her anger reignite if she knew why she had fallen asleep that night? "I forced you to stay here."

"You did? I don't remember that."

"That's because I slipped something into your drink that caused you to fall asleep."

Maren went silent, and I was certain she was about to give me a verbal lashing.

"I see."

An awkward silence stretched between us until we reached the door to our shared chamber.

"I understand if you hate me now," I whispered.

"Oh, Eldwin. I could never hate you. You are not perfect, but neither am I. I tried to make a decision that would affect both our lives without even stopping to consider your thoughts."

She turned to face me, and I saw her eyes were wet with tears. A host of emotions rose within me, and though I tried desperately to hold them back, they poured forth as tears. I buried my head into her shoulder and sobbed. She clung tightly to me, and we shared a moment unlike any we'd experienced before.

I don't know how long we stood like that, but eventually, we released one another and wordlessly entered our room. I pulled my boots off and removed my dirty clothes, climbing into bed with only my undergarments on. Maren scooted close to me, and I fell asleep almost instantly.

The clanging of a bell startled me, and I looked at the window. Light streamed through the stained glass, bathing the floor in a spectrum of colors.

"What is that?" Maren asked, sitting up.

"It's the bell, but it shouldn't be going off now."

We exchanged looks, and as if reading each other's minds, we leaped out of bed and got dressed, hurrying through the halls. We passed Surrel, and I looked over at her questioningly.

"Any idea what's going on?"

"I'm afraid not."

I nodded, and we picked up the pace, joining a small group who were heading for the front entrance of the school. No one seemed to know what the bell was for, and as we stepped into the courtyard, I spotted Anesko. Even he seemed confused. A guard from the walls rushed down the rampart steps and skidded to a halt in front of him.

"Is the enemy leaving?" Anesko asked.

"No, sir. Heralds are approaching under a white banner," the guard huffed.

Maren and I joined them, and Curate Henrik wasn't far behind us.

"Perhaps they've come to announce their withdraw," Henrik suggested.

"Yes, perhaps," Anesko sagely nodded. "I am surprised the encampment is not overcome with chaos by now. If the generals have learned of the king's death, they should be fighting for power."

"All seems calm so far," the guard replied.

"Let us see what they want, then."

We hurried to the ramparts and watched as the heralds approached. The distance made it difficult to see their faces, but I counted at least a dozen men.

"Why so many to announce a withdraw?" I asked.

No one answered, but I didn't expect anyone to. Once the group was just outside the range of our archers, they stopped and waved their banners back and forth.

"I will go out and speak with them," Anesko announced.

"What if it's a trap?" Henrik asked.

"Not even the late king would dare violate the white flag."

While I doubted that was true, it didn't feel right for Anesko to go out there alone. I laid a hand on his shoulder.

"I'm coming with you."

"As am I," Maren said.

"Then we shall go as well." Katori motioned to herself and Henrik.

"You two stay here," Anesko replied, looking at them. "Eldwin and Maren will be plenty."

The three of us returned to the courtyard and waited for the men in the guardhouse to open the southern gates. If it was a trap, at least the enemy would have some trouble with us before they reached Autumnwick.

Three horses were brought for us, and we waited for the barrier to be removed. The portion covering the gates flickered and faded, and we rode out to meet the heralds. As we drew closer, I noticed that one of them was wearing a dark cape, his face concealed by its hood.

"Hail," Anesko greeted, stopping his mount a dozen paces from the heralds.

"His Majesty wishes to speak with you," one of them said. The front riders made a path for the hooded man, and he flicked the reins in his hand, urging his horse forward slowly.

"I heard the king was dead." Anesko's demeanor suddenly became wary.

The figure pulled his hood back, and my eyes widened in surprise. It was Shadamar.

"Erling is dead, and now I rule over Osnen."

Shadmar turned his gaze to me. "You didn't just kill a king," he said. "You killed a brother."

Many things suddenly made sense, especially the reason for his steadfast devotion to Erling. He turned his attention to Maren.

"Niece."

"Uncle."

My heart was pounding in my chest. Shadamar was Erling's brother. How had I not seen it before? The two bore little resemblance, but still. It was so obvious now that I knew. And I had made him watch as I killed his brother.

"I have come to tell you that I am withdrawing my forces. The kingdom will grieve the loss of her former king, and celebrate the rise of her new one. Savor your victory, for it is a fleeting one. I will return to wipe the Order from the face of Osnen, and not even the history books will mention you."

Shadamar looked at me again. "You told me not to forget what you did. I won't."

He turned his mount around and spurred the beast back toward the camp.

# 16

It took the better part of a week, but eventually, the king's forces left the area, leaving an enormous swath of flattened grass and minor destruction behind. Anesko refused to lower the barrier until he knew for certain the army was gone, so Maren and Katori used their magic to see beyond the walls. They confirmed the enemy was indeed gone, and the barrier was removed.

The same day, a group of cloaked riders arrived, stirring up rumors around the school. It turned out to be the Assembly members, and surprisingly, Risod was among them. Maren and I joined Anesko for a meeting with them in the library, as there wasn't enough room in his chambers for all of us.

"I am glad to see that Risod is safe," I said, looking at her with concern. She was obviously exhausted, but her tired expression did little to mute her fierceness. She nodded her head in thanks.

"I am confused how you found her, though, considering you did not follow me to where the slayers held her captive." I kept my tone friendly and tried not to make the words sound like an accusation. Had they shown up, things would have gone much differently.

"I am sorry for deceiving you," Nemryth said. "I wanted to be sure you were not unknowingly leading us into a trap, and we waited to make our appearance. When we did, there was nothing but corpses waiting for us."

"The work of Erling's sorcerer, who is also his brother. Your aid would have been helpful, but I understand why you chose not to make your presence known immediately."

"I trust you have no ill feelings toward us?" she asked.

"No. Things worked out in the end. As well as can be expected, anyway."

Anesko cleared his throat. "Were you able to eliminate the rest of the dragon slayers?"

"As far as we know," Nemryth replied. "There weren't many left based on my count, but if any escaped, it would have only been one or two of them."

"Good. I am glad to be rid of at least one problem." Anesko leaned back against his chair and rubbed his temples.

"That is the reason we have come here. The more I consider their random appearance, the more I cannot believe that they came here accidentally. We must consider the possibility that they were scouts from a larger force. That, or they were sent here to find us specifically."

"What do you mean?" Anesko asked. "They knew who you are?"

"Risod said they interrogated her endlessly, wanting to know where the temple was, among other things. She is strong and told them nothing, but to answer your question, yes, they seemed to know who the Assembly was."

"I don't mean to sound rude, but how is that our problem?"

Nemryth's expression turned into a scowl for only a moment before she composed herself.

"If more of them come, then it will be your problem because they will hunt your dragons. The Order is already on the brink of disaster, and if the Order falls, all of dragon kind will be in danger."

Silence followed, and I heaved a sigh before speaking.

"The wild dragons are still here. Perhaps they have changed their mind about leaving."

"They haven't," Anesko said. "I spoke with Getarros this morning. They will be gone before the day is over. We cannot rely on them."

I had hoped they would stay, but I was not surprised. Dragons were stubborn creatures.

"If I may be so bold as to ask, will the Assembly support us when the king resumes his war?" I asked.

Anesko snapped his head around to look at me, his eyes wide with shock. I wasn't trying to step on his toes, but I wanted to know. After all I had done for them, it was the least they could do.

Nemryth smiled at me.

"Ages ago, we agreed to let our kind bond with yours. For a long time, I was disappointed in our decision, thinking that men were selfish and undeserving of the bond, yet I have come to see that is not true of all of you. The Assembly will support the Order, even in war."

"Thank you," Anesko said, bowing his head. "With our combined efforts, I have hope we will prevail against our enemies, wherever they come from."

"With that said, I have a request."

"Speak it."

"The Assembly has decided to be part of this world. We ask that you allow us to live here at the Citadel with you. It is long overdue for us to leave our temple."

"Granted," Anesko said without hesitation.

"Thank you. This is a new beginning."

I considered Anesko's words as I stood on the ramparts of the wall. They struck a chord within me, and I knew they rang truer than any of us could yet realize. With the Assembly on our side, I was just as confident as Anesko that we could overcome any adversity. Perhaps that would eventually convince Getarros and the other wild dragons to change course and join the Order. Or perhaps we would find more dragons among the black-market traders. Or, to be even more hopeful, perhaps those who had previously provided dragons to the school would soon do so again.

Only time would reveal the next twist on our path, but I was determined to march forward with optimistic steps. I took a deep breath and stared into the distance, filled with a sense of hope and conviction. I was ready to fight for our future, and I would go to the ends of the world if I had to.

*Whatever it takes,* Sion said.

*Whatever it takes,* I replied.


THE END OF BOOK 14

# ABOUT THE AUTHOR

Richard Fierce is a fantasy and space opera author. He's been writing since childhood, but began publishing in 2007. Since then, he's written multiple novels and short stories.

In 2000, Richard won Poet of the Year for his poem *The Darkness*. He's also one of the creative brains behind the Allatoona Book Festival, a literary event in Acworth, Georgia.

A recovering retail worker, he now works in the tech industry when he's not busy writing.

He's married and has three step-daughters (pray for him), three dogs (huskies!), a cat, and two ferrets. He basically has a zoo.

His love affair with fantasy was born in high school when a friend's mother gave him a copy of *Dragons of Spring Dawning* by Margaret Weis and Tracy Hickman.

www.ingramcontent.com/pod-product-compliance
Lightning Source LLC
Chambersburg PA
CBHW061457210726
48287CB00007B/2555